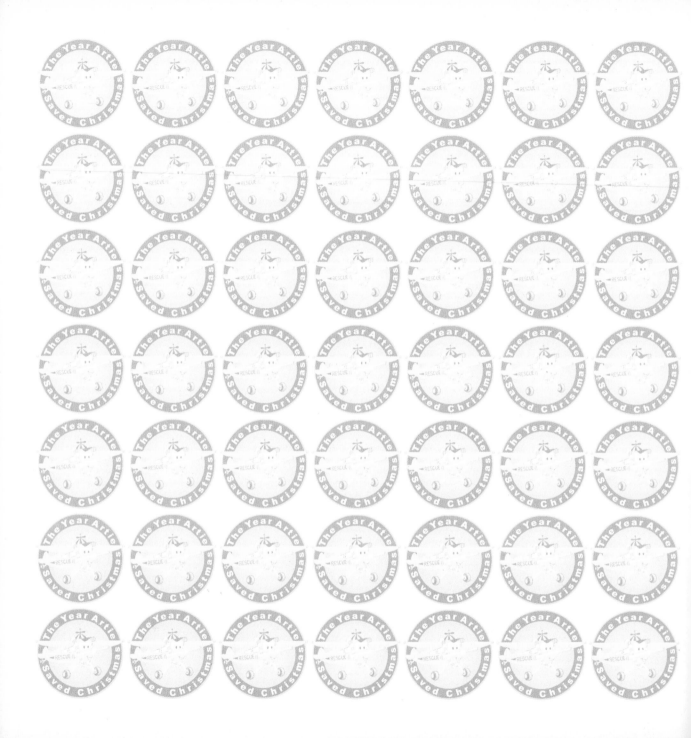

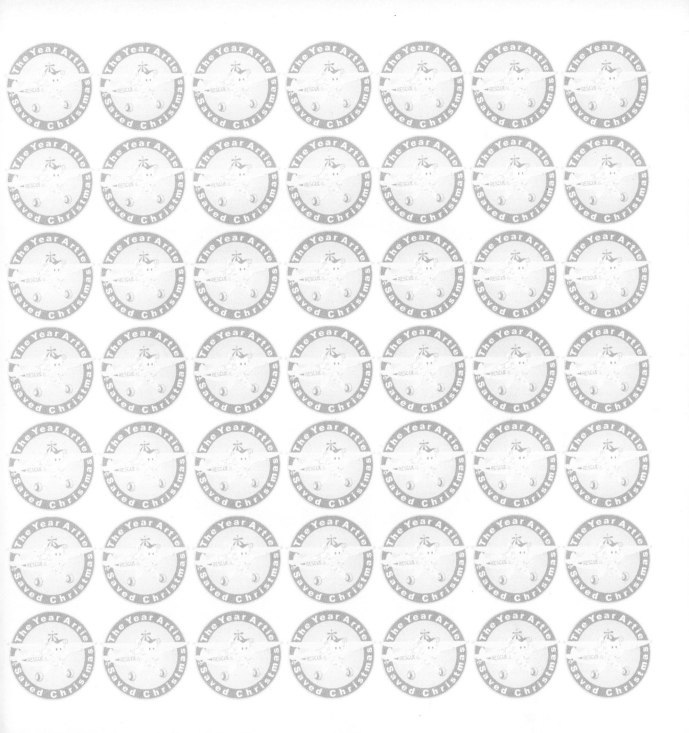

The adventures of
Artie the Airplane
and his friends™

The Year Artie
Saved Christmas

Written and Illustrated
by
Captain Chuck Harman

Christmas! What a wonderful time of the year. Everyone has the holiday spirit. People and planes hurry about getting everything ready for the big day. All of the airports are jammed with people traveling. There are decorations everywhere, changing the look of everything.

This particular year, the day before Christmas was cold and stormy. Almost everyone was inside putting the finishing touches on all of the presents they would give away on Christmas day.

Gramma Cubbie was busy baking cookies and cakes and making a big meal for all the planes at the Big Town airport. Everyone at the Big Town airport loved Gramma Cubbie's Christmas feast! There was excitement in the air.

Artie had finished all of his shopping and was inside his warm hangar wrapping the presents that he had bought or made for his friends.

Artie wrapped the new tires he got for his friend, Jack, and placed them under the tree. Then, Artie wrapped the new sunglasses he got for Frankie. "Frankie will look great in these," he thought.

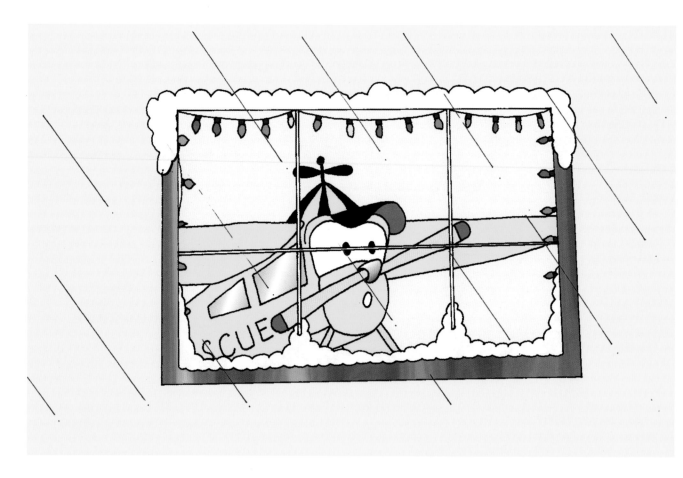

Artie looked out of the big window in his hangar. "Boy, it sure is snowing hard out there," Artie said. "Not a good day for flying at all. I hope nobody needs me tonight!"

Artie was just about ready to go to sleep when, suddenly, the rescue phone rang. "Uh-oh, someone must be in trouble," Artie thought. A rescue worker came running into the hangar to tell Artie that the call was from the North Pole. There was an emergency and Artie was needed there right away.

Artie got ready for the rescue mission. He packed up all of the supplies he thought he would need and put on a scarf to keep warm in the storm.

Artie took off and turned toward the north. "Boy, this snow is bad," he thought. "I'll bet it's snowing pretty hard up at the North Pole. I wonder who needs me? I didn't know people lived up there. I thought only Santa Claus and his Elves lived at the North Pole. . . .Wait a minute. . . . No! It can't be! Santa Claus has called for me?"

When Artie landed, sure enough, Santa Claus was there to meet him. "Thank goodness you're here, Artie. We were worried that it was snowing too hard. I don't know what we would have done if you hadn't made it."

"What's the problem, Santa?" asked Artie. "What can I do to help?"

"Artie," said Santa. "Rudolph has a terrible cold and can't fly."
Santa continued, "Even though this is a very bad storm, all of
the children in the world will still be expecting their toys
tonight and we can't let them down. We can't make it through
this storm without your help. We need you to guide us through
the snow tonight."

Artie couldn't believe it. Santa was asking him to help. Artie said, "I would be happy to help Santa, but how can I take Rudolph's place? Tell me what you need me to do." Santa told Artie that he wanted him to fly in the front of the sleigh and use his radar to guide them through the storm. Rudolph would stay at home with Mrs. Claus and try to get better.

Artie hooked up to the very front of the sleigh and flew all night, using his radar to guide Santa and his reindeer through the storm to every house on Santa's list. Before dawn, the storm let up and Artie finally flew home.

On Christmas morning, Jack and Frankie stopped by Artie's hangar to wish him a Merry Christmas and to exchange gifts with him. When they opened the hangar doors, Artie was fast asleep.

"Merry Christmas, Artie," said Jack.

"Look, it snowed pretty hard last night," said Frankie, "but Santa got through anyway!"

Artie just yawned and smiled at Frankie and said, "Yes, he sure did. I'm glad you came by. Come on in, guys. Merry Christmas."

Jack said, "Artie, you look really tired. Did you have a rescue last night?"

"Yes, I did, Jack," said Artie. "I had to fly all night long and I'm still really tired, but I'm too excited to sleep. Let's open up our presents!"

The three friends spent the day opening up presents and enjoying Gramma Cubbie's special Christmas cookies. Artie never said anything about the rescue on Christmas Eve, but Jack knew that whatever Artie did last night, it must have been pretty special.

That afternoon, as Artie watched his friends taxi away, he thought, "This was the best Christmas ever."

Up at the North Pole, Mrs. Claus brought Rudolph another bowl of soup.

Santa Claus was sitting in his big chair by the fire. He was just finishing up writing about this Christmas in his journal. On the top of the page he had written, "This was the year that Artie saved Christmas."

Meet a few of

Alice the Air Ambulance

Albert T. Agplane

Becky the Big Tire Blimp

Bubba the Bush Plane

Carlos the Cargo Plane

Codi the Copter

Eduardo the Explorer

Frankie the Fighter

Gilda the Glider

Gramma Cubbie

Grampa Cubbie

Heidi the High Wing

Jack the Jumbo

Jessie the Jet Fuel Truck

Leslie the Low Wing

Artie's friends.

Pete the Patrol Car

Pierre the Plane

Piper

Robert the Rescue Plane

Lt. Sam Sweptwing

San Antonio Sal

Simon the Starfighter

Shirley the Skyvan

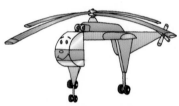

Sigmund the Skycrane

Superslim

Tina the Tailwheel

Waldo W. Wing

Wally the Widebody

Bartholomew T. Barnstormer

Captain Chuck

A Word From Captain Chuck

Hi kids! Thank you for reading my book. All of the lessons in the book series, ***The adventures of Artie the Airplane and his friends***™, will help you grow up to be the best person you can be.

Always remember to eat right, exercise, get plenty of rest and do your very best in school. If you do, you can be whatever you want to be when you grow up.

Visit Artie and me on the net at www.artietheairplane.com

Artiefacts™

A typical international flight on a long-range jetliner uses more than 5 1/2 tons of food service items. These same jetliners carry as much as 57,000 gallons of fuel. If poured into an olympic-sized pool, it would fill it halfway up!

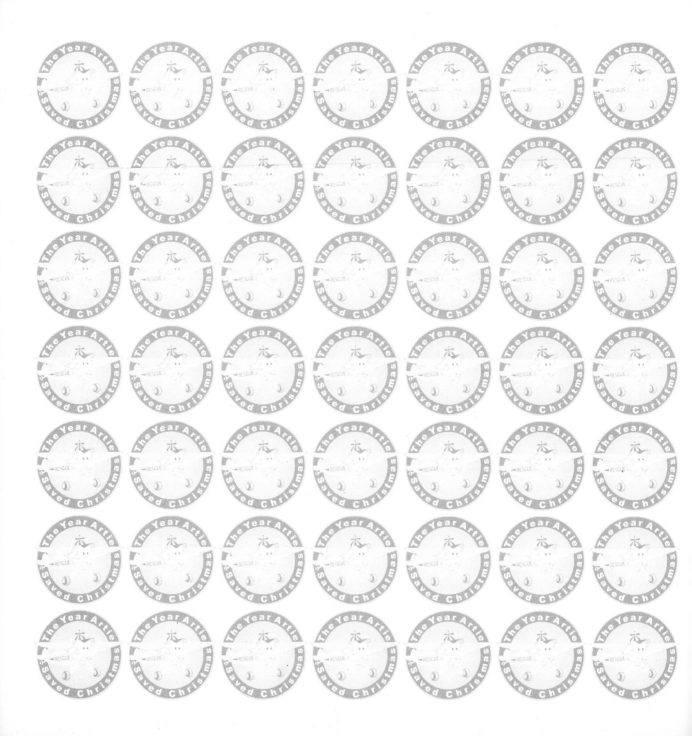